Sapphire's
Special Power

Also by Daisy Sunshine

Twilight, Say Cheese!

UNICORN
University

Sapphire's
Special Power

★ by DAISY SUNSHINE ★
illustrated by MONIQUE DONG

ALADDIN
New York London Toronto Sydney New Delhi

ALADDIN

An imprint of Simon & Schuster Children's Publishing Division

1230 Avenue of the Americas, New York, New York 10020

First Aladdin paperback edition February 2021

Text copyright © 2021 by Simon & Schuster

Illustrations copyright © 2021 by Monique Dong

Also available in an Aladdin hardcover edition.

All rights reserved, including the right of reproduction in whole or in part in any form.

ALADDIN and related logo are registered trademarks of Simon & Schuster, Inc.

For information about special discounts for bulk purchases, please contact Simon & Schuster Special Sales at 1-866-506-1949 or business@simonandschuster.com.

The Simon & Schuster Speakers Bureau can bring authors to your live event. For more information or to book an event contact the Simon & Schuster Speakers Bureau at 1-866-248-3049 or visit our website at www.simonspeakers.com.

Book designed by Laura Lyn DiSiena

The illustrations for this book were rendered digitally.

The text of this book was set in Tinos.

Manufactured in the United States of America 0121 OFF

2 4 6 8 10 9 7 5 3 1

Library of Congress Cataloging-in-Publication Data

Names: Sunshine, Daisy, author. | Dong, Monique, illustrator.

Title: Sapphire's special power / by Daisy Sunshine ; illustrated by Monique Dong.

Description: First Aladdin paperback edition. | New York : Aladdin, 2021. |
Series: Unicorn University ; [2] | Summary: As magical power develops in the last of
her friends, Sapphire fears she will never get hers but maybe she already unlocked
her special magical gift, and just has to find it.

Identifiers: LCCN 2020034015 (print) | LCCN 2020034016 (ebook) |
ISBN 9781534461697 (hardcover) | ISBN 9781534461680 (trade paperback) |
ISBN 9781534461703 (ebook)

Subjects: CYAC: Unicorns—Fiction. | Ability—Fiction. | Magic—Fiction. |
Fairies—Fiction. | Boarding schools—Fiction. | Schools—Fiction.

Classification: LCC PZ7.1.S867 Sap 2021 (print) | LCC PZ7.1.S867 (ebook) | DDC [Fic]—dc23

LC record available at https://lccn.loc.gov/2020034015

LC ebook record available at https://lccn.loc.gov/2020034016

For lovers of sparkles, rainbows, and magic

CONTENTS

1

The Royal Messenger

Sapphire was so excited that she couldn't stop moving. It felt like her hooves were filled with dancing beans. She dashed among her fellow first years of Unicorn University, making sure everyone was ready to go. They were all gathered together on the Looping Lawn, under the two tallest oak trees. The large knobbly branches stretched out far above them, covering the rainbow cluster of unicorn students.

Sapphire noticed that the sun was lower in the sky. She straightened her shoulders and shook her long, braided blue mane. "Okay!" she shouted to get everyone's attention. "Let's get into our places. Shamrock, Firefly, you guys head across the field to make sure the banner is high enough so that Fairy Green can see it when she flies in."

Shamrock, a mint-green colt and one of Sapphire's closest friends, nodded so enthusiastically that his large, black-rimmed glasses went crooked. Using her horn, Sapphire straightened them for him and then held out a large conch shell on a string. "I borrowed this from gym class. Just yell into it, and we'll be able to hear you from across the lawn." Shamrock slipped his horn through the string and straightened his neck so that the string fell down around his shoulders.

"Wow, cool, just like Coach Ruby!" said Firefly, a red-and-gold unicorn.

Sapphire watched Shamrock and Firefly run across the field. She still couldn't believe they were all going to meet a real fairy tomorrow. Fairies lived throughout the five kingdoms, but as royal messengers they usually only appeared to deliver important notes or news. So you didn't meet them unless you were someone super important. But when Sapphire's teacher, Professor Sherbet, had heard that her close friend Fairy Green was traveling through Sunshine

Springs for the annual Fairy Gathering, the professor had asked if her friend could stop by to talk to the first-year students.

Ever since she was little, Sapphire had wanted to travel the five kingdoms. Growing up by the ocean, she'd seen ships travel by from all over the world. She would spend hours at her bedroom window, wondering where they were going and why. But the ships were always just out of reach, close enough to dream about but too far away for Sapphire to talk to anyone on board. So she couldn't help but feel like this meeting with Fairy Green was the start of something very big. As her good friend Twilight would say, it felt like pixies were dancing in her stomach.

It was time for stage two of the Welcome Plan. Sapphire turned to a snow-white unicorn with a red-and-white striped mane named Peppermint, and to a three-legged gray unicorn named Storm. "Okay. Is the banner ready?" Sapphire asked.

The banner certainly looked ready. Sapphire marveled at how Peppermint and Storm had managed to arrange the flowers so that they spelled out WELCOME TO UU, FAIRY

GREEN! They used bright flowers for the letters and green plants for the background. Sapphire noticed that all the flowers had the same shimmer. Curious, she leaned in closer.

"I used my ability with weather to make it shine like that," Storm said proudly. "I protected the morning dew so it wouldn't dry up with the sun."

"Great work, Storm," Sapphire said with a nod of approval.

Peppermint scoffed and flipped her mane. "Well, I used my weaving ability to knit the flowers all together. We wouldn't even have a banner without me," she whined.

"Oh, it's really glitter-tastic! You guys make a fantastic team!" Comet assured her. Sapphire nudged her rose-colored friend with her flank. Comet was always so positive and encouraging. She always made everyone feel like they were part of things, like they belonged. Sapphire loved that about Comet.

"It's absolutely perfect," Sapphire agreed.

Peppermint and Storm grinned and tapped their horns together in a high-U.

"Okay, Comet," Sapphire said. "You're up next!"

Comet had woven fairy's thread through her mane, and it glittered in the bright afternoon sun. But despite all the sparkle, Comet suddenly seemed rather dull. Her eyebrows were scrunched and her mouth twisted to the side. It was a look that was certainly unusual for cheerful Comet.

"What's wrong?" Sapphire asked, her own eyebrows arching with concern.

Comet hoofed the grass beneath her. "It's just, well, I'm nervous about my part. I'm sure I can fly up to the top of the trees, no problem, and I bet I can manage to tie the ropes to the trees. Just . . . what if I can't get back down again?"

Comet had the gift of flight, but she was still learning and had a hard time with her landings. She almost never made it back down without a teacher to help. But they had all agreed to enact the Welcome Plan on their own, no grown-ups allowed.

Sapphire smiled at her sparkly friend. She knew just what to do.

"Peppermint!" Sapphire called—perhaps a little too loudly. Peppermint was right next to her, after all. "Could you weave some ivy around Comet?"

"Um, totes. That's so easy," Peppermint said with her signature mane flip. The red-and-white strands of her mane twisted and twirled together like a bunch of little candy canes. Sapphire couldn't help but admire it.

"Great," Sapphire said. "How about you wrap ivy around Comet's waist, and leave a lot of extra so I can hold one end while Comet flies up to the trees. Then, Comet, when you're ready, we'll just pull you back down again!"

A huge smile with bright pink dimples immediately replaced Comet's frown. "Let's do this!" she cheered.

"Woo-hoo!" Sapphire joined in, followed by enthusiastic whoops from Peppermint and Storm.

Before long the beautiful banner was hung between the oak trees. After finding the right height, Shamrock and Firefly ran over to the group.

The unicorns admired their work. Sapphire was proud of her classmates for pulling it all off. She thought about her own first day at Unicorn University and the rainbow banner that had welcomed the first year students. She wanted to make sure Fairy Green felt just as welcome.

"And now for the final step," Sapphire said. "Twilight, do you have the Spotlight Flowers?"

Twilight was another one of Sapphire's best friends, and she had the gift of invisibility. Spotlight Flowers were found only in one patch of field on campus, and from afar you could see their giant heads lifting up and casting beams of different-colored lights. Students loved to go up to the Magic Meadow to watch the Spotlight Flowers in the evening, as the flowers seemed to respond to each other and it was like watching lights dance. But whenever anyone got close, the flowers would curl up and disguise themselves as weeds, making it impossible to tell which was the disguised Spotlight Flower and which was a regular old weed.

That was, until Sapphire and Comet had hatched a plan. It had taken some convincing to get Twilight and Shamrock on board, but eventually they'd figured out that Twilight's invisibility allowed her to sneak into the fields so that the flowers wouldn't know a thing. When Sapphire had dreamt up the welcome banner, she'd known just how to make sure Fairy Green would see the banner even if she flew in at night. The Spotlight Flowers would make the perfect royal welcome. Luckily, Twilight had agreed to gather a basketful of the special plants to replant under the big oak trees.

But looking around now, Sapphire couldn't see Twilight anywhere. *Oh no*, Sapphire worried. *Is Twilight stuck invisible again?*

2

Bright Lights, Big Banner

Sapphire looked to the stables and was relieved to see Twilight galloping toward the group, but when Twilight got closer, Sapphire could see tears brimming in Twilight's eyes, and her lower lip trembling with worry. "Saph, I can't find the basket anywhere," she said when she stopped short, still panting from the quick pace. "I picked the flowers right after breakfast, but I have no idea where the basket went between then and now!"

A chorus of groans came from the students. Sapphire knew that Twilight hated attention more than anything else, and Twilight's hooves were shimmering in and out of invisibility, which usually meant she was panicking. Sapphire

needed to get everyone to focus elsewhere. And fast.

She jumped into action. "It's okay, guys! We just need to retrace our steps. Who remembers seeing the basket after Twilight came out of the Spotlight Garden?" Sapphire asked.

The whole class erupted like a volcano with thoughts and ideas of where the basket could be. But absolutely no one was listening to the others. It reminded Sapphire of their first day of school, when they'd all been trying to think of a class picture idea.

Then Shamrock blurted out, "The Crystal Library!"

At first Sapphire just thought he meant they should go to the library to figure out the problem. As much as Sapphire loved that magical place, she didn't think the answer was going to be in a book. But when she turned to Shamrock to tell him so, she saw a look in his eyes that she'd never seen before. It was a bit like when he was trying to figure out the answer to a tough question, like he was looking far into the distance. But this look was way more intense. Like he was seeing light-years ahead.

Then Shamrock yelled, "The Peony Pasture!"

That made the whole class pay attention. In fact, everyone stopped talking at once. Shamrock was usually a very calm unicorn, certainly not one to just shout stuff.

Just as suddenly as it had come, Shamrock seemed to jump out of his trance. His face broke into a big, goofy smile that pushed his glasses up to his eyebrows. "Follow me," he told the group in his usual voice. "I know where the flowers are!" And he dashed off in the direction of the Silver Lining Stables, the students' dormitories. The class hurried after him, many asking what had happened, but Shamrock ignored them all.

Shamrock stopped short in front of Twilight's stall, and Sapphire arrived not long after him. She smiled at the photo that always hung below the shiny golden number twelve.

The picture was from their very first day of school, with Sapphire, Comet, Shamrock, and Twilight all posed happily with powdered sugar smudged all over their faces. Sapphire had been so nervous that first day. It had felt like she would never belong. But now, only one month in, she couldn't imagine being anywhere else. She loved everything about Unicorn U.

With Twilight's permission, Shamrock swung open Twilight's door to reveal a basket full of Spotlight Flowers.

"Of course!" Twilight squeaked. "We stopped by here to get some string for the banner, and I must have left the basket behind. Thank you, Shamrock!"

"But how'd you know that?" Storm asked. "Only Twilight and I came by here. Weren't you still out on the lawn?"

"I think I've developed my ability," Shamrock told them, his eyes sparkling with joy. "I think I have a special photographic memory! All of a sudden, I could rewind my day like a—" He stopped short and squinted a little, as if searching for the right word. "Like a memory movie! And I remembered that you had the basket in the Crystal Library but not in the Peony Pasture at lunch, but you did have the string. So it made sense that you would have left the flowers when you got your art supplies from your stall!" he finished happily, and slightly out of breath.

The class cheered and started back up to the giant oak trees, Spotlight Flowers in hand. Sapphire nudged Shamrock on the way, and he looked back at her with a grin. She could tell how happy he was that his special power had finally appeared. And she was happy for her friend.

Once they reached the banner, Sapphire stood back and directed everyone to carefully replant the flowers and, using Twilight's string, aim them to light up the banner with soft blues, pinks, and yellows. It was spectacular.

The dinner bell rang, and Sapphire watched her classmates dash off to the Peony Pasture for apples and oats before bed. But she hung back just a bit to admire their creation one more time. Butterflies danced in her stomach, and she couldn't help but smile with excitement. She was going to meet a fairy tomorrow!

3

Breakfast Dreams

The next morning, Sapphire opened her eyes in time to watch the sun rise from her stall window. The stable was quiet—everyone was surely still sleeping—but Sapphire couldn't go back to sleep. The dancing beans in her hooves were back in full force. The day was finally here! Sapphire crept softy out of her stall, careful not to let the door bang and wake up the other fillies. The seaweed wreath her sisters had sent from home swung quietly as she slowly let the door close behind her. Avoiding all the creaky planks, she made her way out to the fields. The sun was still low in the sky, and the whole campus was bathed in a warm orange and pink light. It felt like a different world, making the morning even more exciting.

When she was far enough away from the stables, Sapphire broke into a quick canter. She raced across the Looping Lawn, the fresh morning dew brushing her blue calves as she ran through the grass. She smiled with delight when she reached their beautiful banner hanging between the oak trees. She felt so proud of their work as she watched the Spotlight Flowers' early-morning light show. Folding her four legs beneath her, she sat down and looked out across the campus. She could see the red barns of the Silver Lining Stables, looking as asleep as its dwellers, and the Crystal Library, the castle-like structure glittering even though the sun was so low.

The view was beautiful, and she was just so comfortable. Right before sleep overtook her, Sapphire saw a green blur in the sky overhead stop short. *Could it be?* Sapphire wondered. *Did I just see Fairy Green? Or am I already dreaming?*

★

Sapphire woke with a start. The sun was now high in the sky, and she could feel that the campus had come alive, the voices of her classmates chattering in the distance. *Have I missed the morning bell?* She quickly got to her hooves, blinking the sleep out of her eyes. Her belly rumbled as she cantered over to the Peony Pasture, hoping to make it in time for breakfast.

She was happy to see her classmates still clustered around their favorite apple tree. She didn't know why they chose it every day, but it was the first place where they had all eaten, and somehow they had silently agreed to gather there ever since.

Sapphire wedged herself between Comet and Twilight and plucked a big, pink apple from the branch above her. She tried to catch up with the morning conversation as she munched.

"I actually developed my ability when I was sleeping," Peppermint was saying. "I had fallen asleep by the fire after I'd been up late reading. I woke with my mother's knitting all stitched around me. I guess sleeping me had wanted a blanket."

Sapphire laughed with the rest of her class, imagining the sight.

But the laughter stopped quickly when a group of older unicorns came up to them. Older unicorns almost never talked to first years. Sapphire gulped the mouthful of apple she'd been chewing and exchanged a questioning look with Comet. Sapphire noticed the other first years were fidgeting around her. Clearly everyone was nervous!

"We just wanted to congratulate you guys on that welcome banner for Fairy Green," said Flash, a hot-pink unicorn with a rainbow mane. Sapphire couldn't believe the captain of the senior hoofball team and basically the coolest unicorn ever was congratulating them on her idea. She could feel her cheeks heat up.

Peppermint tossed her mane with an especially dramatic flair and said, "*I* wove the flowers together. I was just telling everyone about my special abilities."

"And I added the glittering dew," Storm offered.

"And Twilight gathered the Spotlight Flowers because she can turn invisible, and Shamrock found the flowers because of his photographic memory!" Comet added, hovering above the grass a little in her excitement.

"But it wouldn't have been possible without Comet! She flew up and hung the banner for us," Shamrock added.

"And Sapphire—" Twilight started, but she was too quiet for others to hear her.

Flash had started talking again. "Sounds like you guys are the dream team. Your abilities are awesome."

Flash's silver-haired teammate, Chrome, said, "Yeah. You guys are totally the coolest first years that Unicorn U has ever seen. Our biggest project was trying to figure out what ability Headmaster Starblaze had. Definitely not as awesome."

"Oh yeah!" Flash remembered. "Must be something super top secret if no one has discovered it yet."

"You mean you never figured it out?" Shamrock asked.

"Nope," said Chrome. "But hey, if anyone can figure it out, it's you guys."

With that, Chrome and Flash headed out, leaving the first-year students in a happy glow.

Sapphire just shrugged and turned back to her break-fast. Why were they talking about the boring old headmaster when they could have been talking about the royal messenger who was eating with their teachers *right now*? Sapphire looked over to see a small green figure sitting on one of the low branches at the teachers' tree. The fairy and Professor Sherbet were leaning in close together, laughing hysterically. Sapphire wondered what they were talking about. Could it be one of their adventures? Sapphire imagined herself sitting at the teachers' tree, all grown up and laughing about her own explorations. "And that's what happens when you mistake a mermaid for a sea serpent!" she imagined herself saying, to a chorus of laughter.

"Hey, Saph," Twilight said, drawing her friend back to the present.

Sapphire shook herself loose from the daydream. "Yeah, Twilight?"

"Did you forget your notebook? I can go back to the stables with you. I have to get my paints, anyway."

"Twilight, you genius!" Sapphire hung her long neck around Twilight in a hug. She was happy her friend had reminded her of her brand-new notebook. Sapphire had asked her mom to send it to her when she'd found out that Fairy Green was coming. She wanted to record everything the fairy said. This was the start of Sapphire's dreams coming true!

4

Meeting Ms. Green

After getting Sapphire's notebook and Twilight's paints, the two unicorns hurried to the Magic Meadow to meet up with their class. The Meadow was farther out on campus and was used a lot less than other spaces, but Sapphire thought it was one of the most beautiful places at Unicorn U.

When they arrived, Twilight and Sapphire could see that the rest of the class had already gathered under the large weeping willow. It's long, delicate branches and dark green leaves hung around the students like curtains. Some branches extended over the stream bank, and some dipped into the glittering water. Everyone was clustered around

Professor Sherbet, who stood next to a tall tree stump. When Twilight and Sapphire joined the group, they could see that Fairy Green was perched atop the stump, which allowed her to look at them at eye level. Her wings were made of what appeared to be large, green leaves, and her hair was piled high atop her head in a swirl that reminded Sapphire of the drippy sandcastles she would build at the beach. Fairy Green's face and hands were forest green, and her dress was made of different types of moss, all woven together in

a striped pattern. *Fairy Green looks like she's part of the meadow,* Sapphire thought.

"Hello, students!" Professor Sherbet called out in her usual warm and friendly way. Today the professor wore a crown made of moss that looked just like the moss of Fairy Green's dress. "I am so excited to introduce you all to my very good friend, the one and only Fairy Green! Please gather round while she tells us some things about her life, and later we can ask her some questions."

Fairy Green flew smoothly from her perch and hovered in front of the students. Now she was slightly above them, making the very air her stage. "Thank you, my friend," she said, turning to Professor Sherbet. It was clear the two had known each other for a long time. Sapphire hoped she would stay friends with Twilight, Comet, and Shamrock for just as long. "And thank you, students, for the wonderful banner! I've been all over the world, but I've never felt so welcome." She paused to smile at them all. Sapphire could feel her heart swell with pride.

"I'm on my way to the annual Fairy Gathering," Fairy

Green continued. Her voice was much louder than one would expect, given her size. She was as loud as any unicorn, or even a dragon. "It is my favorite time of the year, for it is when fairies throughout the five kingdoms come together in our Woodland City to meet to discuss the world's news. There are parties and so much music! It is the true meaning of magic." Her forest-green eyes lit up when she spoke. "There are lots of different types of fairies with different types of magic. We may seem very different from you but unicorns and fairies have something very important in common. Does anyone know what that is?" She let the question hang in the air as the first years struggled to figure out what she meant.

Sapphire's heart soared as she raised her horn. She knew just what Fairy Green meant.

"Yes, you with the magnificent blue coat," Fairy Green called out.

"Hello, Fairy Green. My name is Sapphire," she said in a loud, clear voice. "Like unicorns, fairies draw their magic from the Four Magical Elements."

Professor Sherbet neighed merrily, clearly proud of her pupil.

Fairy Green clapped her hands together softly, filling the air with the sound of rustling leaves. "Very good, Sapphire!"

Sapphire felt as if she were floating on the ocean, buoyed up by happiness. This was the best day of her life.

"All fairies draw their strength from one of the Four Magical Elements: light, water, earth, and air. As a Forest Fairy, I am most connected to the earth element. But I do have wings, and while they are not as strong as the Flight Fairies' wings, I am connected to the air as well. Just as you unicorns, no matter where your ability comes from, are connected to all four elements too." Fairy Green paused again to let the words sink in.

"Both unicorns and fairies come from Sunshine Springs," she continued. "And so we all share a very special connection and friendship, one that goes back thousands and thousands of years. Does anyone know this story?"

This time it was Shamrock's turn to wave his horn in the air. He was so enthusiastic that it was surprising he managed to keep his glasses on straight. Fairy Green gestured for him to answer.

"I have read only a little about this," Shamrock began, "but I think it has something to do with your basket of fairy dust? Unicorns and fairies found it together."

Sapphire nodded as he spoke. She and Shamrock had been doing some research and they had read this in one of the books the librarian, Professor Jazz had recommended.

"Your unicorns are very quick, Professor Sherbet!" Fairy Green turned to her friend with a smile. "I see great things for your class."

Professor Sherbet beamed.

"Quite right, Shamrock," Fairy Green said. "Long ago, fairies and unicorns sent out an expedition team to map all of Sunshine Springs, and this team found the Sacred Forest. You see, at one time all the fairies lived in different parts of our kingdom, not in the four sacred cities as we do today, and together they found the Tree of Knowledge. Legend has it that the pollen swirled and covered the team completely. It looked as if powdered sugar had rained from the heavens."

Fairy Green gave them all a little wink. Clearly Professor Sherbet had told her the story of their class picture.

Sapphire looked over to Twilight, who was blushing but still had a big smile on her face. The rest of the class was laughing along.

"The pollen made the unicorns sneeze, but to the fairies it was magic. We learned that it would make us stronger. And would allow us to travel far distances without wearing out our wings. I can't tell you how, as we fairies have *some* secrets, but it is only with this basket that I am able to travel the five kingdoms. You may know this pollen as fairy dust." She flew back to her stump to pick up her basket. It was made of a deep brown bark with a lid that fit perfectly, and a long strap made of woven ivy that allowed her to carry it over her shoulder. Putting the basket down, she resumed her story. "The unicorns helped us build our city around the tree, which would become the Woodland City and our capital. In return, the fairies brought builders from throughout the five kingdoms and helped create libraries, like your Crystal Library, all over Sunshine Springs. The unicorns wanted to record all that they learn from us, and from all the other creatures of the five kingdoms for generations to come."

The students started chattering immediately after Fairy Green had stopped speaking. They'd had no idea that this was where the libraries had come from. Sapphire couldn't wait to discuss it with Professor Jazz, later.

"Okay. I think it's about time for questions!" Fairy Green said, and she was met with an immediate wave of horns. The first years wiggled and jumped to be called on, looking like a rainbow flag waving together. Sapphire thought about all the questions she wanted to ask. Comet was called on first, probably because she had hovered so high in her excitement that Shamrock had to pull her down by her tail. "Is 'Fairy Green' your real name? It seems sorta plain for you, if you don't mind me saying."

Fairy Green chuckled, and Sapphire thought it sounded just like a swirl of leaves whipping together in the wind. "Very good question. No, 'Fairy Green' is not my full name. It's the name I use when traveling. My real name is known by all fairies, but I share it with only very few other creatures, for it holds great power. Does anyone else have a question?"

Fairy Green answered all their questions, from "Where do fairies sleep?" (in hammocks) to "What is your favorite kingdom to visit?" (Soaring Spires) to "Do you ever travel by bird?" (She did when she was too young use fairy dust).

Sapphire was swept away by it all, making mental notes to record later in her notebook. Her mouth hung slightly open, and she only noticed that a little bit of drool had escaped when she was called on for the last question.

"I believe the final question should go to Sapphire, since she answered my first question. And I do love symmetry," Fairy Green said smartly.

"You said that you have

to use fairy dust to travel the five kingdoms. Does everyone have to have something magical in order to explore?" Sapphire felt good about this question. She'd have to know what she'd need to be an explorer, and she truthfully didn't know where to start.

"You know, no one has ever asked me that before," Fairy Green told her. Then she paused for much longer than she had for the other questions. "Yes," she said finally. "I do believe all creatures who travel widely must possess a certain type of magic."

"Like a magical ability?" Peppermint asked.

"Yes, I suppose so. Something like that," Fairy Green answered.

Those words hit Sapphire like a bag of crystal bricks.

But I don't have a magical ability, she thought.

Professor Sherbet thanked Fairy Green and dismissed the first years to their break, but Sapphire couldn't hear any of it. It felt like pixies were buzzing in her ears, repeating what Fairy Green had said. *There can never be any explor-*

ing for me, thought Sapphire. Tears welled up and threatened to fall.

Out of the corner of her eye, she saw Comet, Twilight, and Shamrock move toward her with sad looks on the faces, but Sapphire just shook her head and walked farther into the meadow.

5

Taking Flight

Sapphire decided to run. She ran as fast as she could through the low stream, feeling the cool water splash around her hooves. It cleared her head, and soon enough she had a thought.

I just have to find my magic.

Sapphire stopped abruptly, causing the water to form a wave big enough to splash onto her chest, cooling her off. After stepping out of the stream and shaking the water off her flanks, Sapphire headed up the grassy bank. She thought all about what Fairy Green had said, and how fairies had not had the magic to travel before they'd found the special pollen. After that, they'd been able to go anywhere. Even her friends hadn't had magic before they'd discovered their abilities. What if Sapphire had simply not found her ability yet? After all, she'd never cared to search for one before. Perhaps she just had to give her ability an extra push. Then she'd have the magic she needed to reach her dreams.

Using her horn, Sapphire pulled her new notebook from the bag that hung around her shoulders, and laid the book out in front of her. *This will be called my quest book*, she thought. Then she took out the little inkwell. The notebook was plain, just made of a simple bark, but the inkwell was spectacular. It was made from an extra large pearl that had been hollowed out. Sapphire pulled the cork stopper out with her teeth before dipping her horn into the bright blue ink. It was a little awkward, writing without a desk, but she decided to go for it anyway.

Very carefully Sapphire wrote "The Magic Quest" at the top of the page. But then she paused. *Where do I start?* she wondered.

Sapphire's mother could breathe underwater by asking air bubbles to come together to create a sort of helmet around her. She harvested seaweed, and this ability with air was very helpful. Sapphire wondered if she had some sort of air gift as well. Maybe she could even fly! That would be the perfect way to explore. She could simply fly to all the five kingdoms, like a fairy! Sapphire decided to find Comet to see if her flying friend could help her unlock this ability.

Sapphire was so excited to have a plan that she felt like singing. She dipped her horn into the ink once again and, under the title, wrote "Learn to fly."

After packing up her bag again, Sapphire skipped to the Friendly Fields. Luckily, she and Comet had hoofball practice together, so it was perfect timing.

Coach Ruby was blowing her final huddle-up whistle as Sapphire joined the group. She and Comet were on the junior hoofball team, made up of first and second years.

In the spring they would play junior hoofball teams from other schools in Sunshine Springs. Sapphire had joined the team because she loved playing with her sisters and cousins at home, and she was usually the MVU (Most Valuable Unicorn) when they played over the holidays. Comet had decided to join the team too because she thought it would be fun to run around all day. Plus, she liked the uniforms.

Sapphire saw Flash directing the senior hoofball team on the other side of the arena, in complicated plays Sapphire didn't recognize. The junior team was still learning the basics.

"Pair up, everyone," Coach Ruby said. "I want you all to find your hoofball strengths this week. We'll be doing some practice games next week, and you all should figure out which positions you'd like to try. If you love to kick, and can kick in the right direction, think about being a forward. If you like the horn toss, think about being goalie. If you love to run, think about defense. And if you have questions, ask." Coach Ruby blew her conch shell horn once in dismissal. Sapphire liked Coach Ruby. She always got to the point quickly.

Sapphire and Comet walked away from the group and started passing the hoofball back and forth, warming up.

"Comet," Sapphire said, trapping the ball underneath her front right hoof. "What do you think about figuring out our strengths a little differently today?"

Recognizing Sapphire's "adventure voice," Comet cheered, "Oh yeah!" And then she said a little more softly, "What do you mean, though?"

"Okay. You know I want to be an explorer more than anything else, right?" Sapphire asked.

Comet nodded. "Of course!"

"Right," Sapphire said. "But Fairy Green said I'd need magic."

"Yeah, but, Saph—" Comet started to argue.

Sapphire just shook her head and kept going, "Well, I think I just haven't developed my magical ability yet. And it needs a little push, you know?"

"Totally makes sense," Comet said. "I mean, it's not like I started flying randomly. I was baking with my aunt one day, and my oat doughnuts were always getting messed up. Like, I could not figure out how to get the holes round enough so that I could serve them with my horn. Sure, they tasted okay. But I wanted to be able to slip them off my horn onto a plate like the real chefs do."

"Yes . . . ," Sapphire said impatiently, motioning with her horn for Comet to get to the point.

"Right, right," Comet went on. "Well, my whole huge family was over—like, everyone—and it was after dinner and I had put the doughnuts into the oven to be ready for dessert. So I pull them out, and there they are, super round!

Not wanting to mess it up, more calm than I'll, like, ever be again, I slipped them onto my horn and carried them out to the table in the garden. With a perfect flourish I slipped all the doughnuts onto the table, just like a chef! Well, I got so excited, I felt lighter than air. And I just started flying and flying. And that's when I got stuck in a tree. And then my uncle flew up—he has the flight gift too—and got me back down again. But anyway, it was when I was super excited. So, why don't you try thinking about your favorite things?"

So it was all about feeling lighter than air. That made sense to Sapphire. She closed her eyes and took a breath, like Twilight did when she needed to calm herself. Actually, Sapphire was pretty sure that Shamrock had taught her that trick, because he used it when he started going off on a long explanation.

"This is a great idea, Comet. My favorite things. . . . Water and swimming, learning about the five kingdoms, reading," Sapphire started. She felt happy thinking about everything she loved, but not lighter.

"Maybe more specific?" Comet offered.

"What do you mean?" Sapphire asked.

"Think like Twilight. Details," Comet suggested.

Sapphire bit her lip, thinking. "My absolute favorite thing to do is jump from the big rock by our house into the ocean. The best part is before you land in the water. It actually is like flying." Now she definitely felt better, remembering all that. But she still wasn't flying. She looked up at Comet to see her friend with a big, secretive smile on her face.

"You should for sure jump off something," Comet said. "I mean, you basically just described flying. That's what we need to do!"

"Makes sense to me!" Sapphire said. She and Comet tended to just go for things when they were alone together. She wondered what careful Twilight and Shamrock would say. But she shrugged it off. This was the day to take chances. She was discovering her magic!

"What about the bleachers?" Comet suggested.

Sapphire looked over. They didn't seem too high. Not high enough for her to get hurt, anyway. "Perfect," she said.

And that was how Sapphire found herself sprawled on the ground feeling very bruised.

"Sapphire! Are you okay?" Coach Ruby ran toward them from across the field. Even from far away they could feel her concern.

"I'm okay, Coach," Sapphire said, slowly getting back to her hooves, shaking off the fall.

"What in the five kingdoms were you doing?" Coach asked.

"Um, trying to see if I had a jumping strength?" Sapphire tried.

"Well, don't do that again." Coach Ruby laughed a little, relaxing after seeing that her player wasn't hurt. "Why don't you go see Stella and Celest? They can give you a tonic and make sure you're okay."

Stella and Celest did all the cooking for the school, and all the medical stuff, too.

"Oh, can I go too?" Comet asked. She spent a lot of time baking and cooking with them, even if she wasn't technically supposed to.

Coach Ruby shook her head. "Join up with Storm and Peppermint, and try to keep things safe this time."

"Maybe we can try to fly again later?" Comet asked Sapphire after Coach Ruby had left to help another teammate.

Sapphire shrugged. "No. I think we can agree that I do not have the gift of flight. But I wonder if Stella could help. I mean, she's a dragon! She has to know loads about traveling and magic."

Comet jumped up and hovered a little before landing back down with a thud. "Totally!"

Before she left, Sapphire took out her notebook and inkwell again and rested it on one of the benches. She crossed out "Learn to fly" and beneath it wrote, "Ask an expert."

6

Questing

On her way to the kitchens, Sapphire saw Shamrock in the Peony Pasture, examining something on the ground underneath the teachers' tree.

"Curiosity kills the quest." Sapphire sighed to herself, and headed toward Shamrock.

"What's up, Shamrock?" Sapphire stopped next to her friend and looked down where he was looking.

Shamrock jumped back in surprise and whipped his long silver mane around so that he could face Sapphire. Which in turn startled Sapphire, and she jumped back too.

After the giggles stopped, Shamrock put his serious face

back on. "Okay, but don't tell anyone," he said, looking around to make sure they were alone. "I wanted to see the fairy dust for myself, so I came investigating to see if any had leaked out, and sure enough there's a little pile right here. And it really does look just like powdered sugar!"

Sapphire could barely contain her excitement. A pile of magic right there?! She leaned over carefully and held her breath so as not to blow any away. She couldn't help but laugh when she realized what it was. "Shamrock! That looks like powdered sugar because it is!"

"No way. It isn't all sticky like when we used it for the class picture. That was more like paint."

"That's because it was mixed up with Twilight's sweat and, well, tears. This must have fallen off the candied apple Fairy Green was eating."

Shamrock raised his eyebrows. "I don't know . . . ," he began.

So Sapphire licked a little, not too much, in case it really was dust. But sure enough, it was sweet powdered sugar.

"Aw, man," Shamrock groaned. "I was so excited. I guess since I didn't get to go to the kitchens that time, I'm—um—not as familiar with the substance."

Sapphire laughed again. "Well, do you want to go now?" she asked. "Coach Ruby sent me to get a tonic and have a quick look-over to make sure I'm not hurt."

Shamrock looked up with concern, his bushy eyebrows popping out over his thick glasses. "What happened?"

"Oh, I'll explain on the way," Sapphire said.

★

Sapphire had just finished her tale when they reached the kitchen.

"Whoa, cool. I can't wait to see what Stella says. But, Sapphire, I don't think you need magic. I mean, you already can do everything. You're the smartest unicorn I know," Shamrock said.

"That's very nice," she said dismissively. "But I've started the quest for magic, Shamrock. And I need to finish it."

That was the type of logic Shamrock could understand, so he nodded supportively.

Looking up at the large, moss-covered building attached to a giant oak tree, Sapphire felt a rush of warmth. She loved the stitched bark walls and the chimney made of smooth, white pebbles. Of all the places at Unicorn U, this was where Sapphire felt most at home.

Sapphire used her glittering horn to knock three times on the huge oak door. Seconds later it swung open to reveal a smiling Stella and Celest.

"We heard you were coming!" boomed Stella, a small green dragon in a bright pink apron. "Coach Ruby sent a message ahead. But I see you stopped to grab a friend?"

Shamrock held his horn up high and gave her his "best student" look. "I'm Shamrock."

"Of course you are! We're happy to meet you," said Celest, a gray speckled unicorn with a curly, gray mane. "Come, come. It's too nice out for the kitchen," she said as she pushed Stella out the door. "Let's have our exam by the stream here. We even have some candied apples, so we can make a little picnic out of it." Stella held up an overflowing basket as proof.

Sapphire had never had so much fun at a doctor's appointment. Before long, the four of them were settled on a large blue-checkered picnic blanket. And Sapphire was deemed perfectly healthy.

"So, why were you really jumping off those bleachers, Sapphire?" Stella asked. As a dragon, Stella had a different type of magic and tended to see things that others missed. She could even see Twilight when she was fully invisible.

"Because . . . well, in order to become an explorer, I need to find my magic," Sapphire admitted. "Fairy Green said so today."

"I've met a few fairies in my day," Stella said. "But she is my absolute favorite." Stella stretched out and leaned against the tree, folding her scaly arms behind her so that her large head could rest on her hands. Her tail and legs were curled up beneath her.

"But what do you mean, find your magic?" Celest asked.

"My magical ability. Shamrock just discovered his yesterday, and now I'm on a quest to find mine."

Stella and Celest looked at each other, sharing their

special thing. It always seemed as if they could communicate with each other without speaking.

"Why don't we roast some marshmallows?" Celest suggested. "Stella, would you make the fire?"

"Oh! Could you teach me?" Sapphire asked. "That seems like a very important skill for an explorer."

Stella raised her scaly eyebrows in surprise. "No unicorn has ever asked me before! I'd love to." She took her claws from behind her head and sat up taller, clearly pleased by her own new adventure.

Shamrock and Sapphire smiled and inched closer to their dragon friend.

"To start, we'll need wood." Stella began her lesson. "Celest, could you grab some?"

"Of course," Celest agreed, disappearing into the house and quickly reappearing with a bundle of wood tied in an old red cloth. She had carried it with her horn and dumped it a few steps away from the picnic blanket.

Stella rumbled over to the wood, then settled herself on

her hind legs. Shamrock and Sapphire stood up and circled around.

"Every dragon can simply blow on a bundle of wood and make a fire," Stella told them. "But it is important that all of us learn to build a fire as well. It teaches us to respect the fire, which we dragons need for everything from food to building to communication. Fire is a very big deal for dragons."

Sapphire figured it was like water for her family. Everything about her life at home revolved around the ocean.

"Now, there are many ways for dragons to build fires. For example, I have fingers and scales and talons that can spark a flame. But there are hundreds of ways! I know them all."

Sapphire looked down at her hooves. She wasn't sure they would be very helpful.

"But there seems to be only one way a unicorn can build a fire without help," Celest joined in. "After all, we never used fire before the dragons showed us how. And we only really use it for cooking. In the north the long-haired unicorns use it for warmth only on the coldest days."

Shamrock and Sapphire nodded in unison. All the unicorns knew that their stoves were built by dragons, and designed so that the unicorns only needed to turn a little knob and—poof!—fire. And if they didn't have a stove, unicorns would use a special dragon-designed device that would turn sunlight into fire if held the right way.

"I'd love to go up north," Sapphire said. "I've never met a long-haired unicorn before. I wonder what their schools look like."

"I'm sure you'll see for yourself someday," Celest told her.

Stella took up the lesson. "For a unicorn to make a fire, you must have one rock the size of your hoof or bigger."

Celest demonstrated, knocking a big rock in front of her.

Sapphire smiled, watching the two of them. Celest and Stella seemed like one creature, half unicorn, half dragon. They wove their words and actions together like they were each one half of a whole.

"Then," Stella continued, "strike the rock with your horn in a curved motion so that a spark appears. We dragons do this with one of our claws."

Sapphire and Shamrock hurried to find their own rocks, eager to try to make a spark. Sapphire looked around for the perfect one. She figured it should have a flat side to rest on, so it didn't tip over went she struck it with her horn. After a bit of searching, she found exactly what she was looking for.

Celest demonstrated, and a spark appeared just as Stella had described. Sapphire and Shamrock tried to follow but only found themselves making terrible scraping noises against their own rocks.

Wincing at the noise, Celest offered some advice. "Try to make a *C* with your horn, and hit the rock at the very end of the curve."

This made perfect sense to Sapphire, and she did just that. She was pleased to see

a little spark appear in front of her. Shamrock didn't manage to create a spark, but he cheered along with Stella and Celest at Sapphire's success.

"Incredible, Sapphire!" Stella said, pleased with her new student. "I've never seen a unicorn pick that up so quickly. Now you'll need to gather some dried leaves from the ground, and some very small sticks. Add these to the pile of wood. I've already arranged the wood in the perfect pile, but that's a lesson for another day."

Sapphire gathered the required materials while Shamrock continued to work on his spark.

Once everything was put together, Stella continued the lesson. "Okay, now position your rock so the spark will meet with one of the dried materials and then the fire will catch."

Sapphire created a few sparks, and a small fire appeared in front of her. She was so happy, which made her think of Comet's doughnut story. She felt lighter than air.

The little group cheered again. "I am very impressed, Sapphire," Stella said. "You would fit right in with the dragons."

Sapphire grinned. She imagined herself surrounded by dragons, listening to them tell stories around a bonfire.

"Well done! It took me weeks to do it, really," Celest added.

"Thank you for teaching me, Stella and Celest," Sapphire said. "I have to admit, I feel kind of proud of myself."

Smiling, Sapphire took out her notebook and ink, and instead of crossing out "Ask an expert," she put a little check mark next to it. They may not have figured out her a magical ability, but she had learned something new.

7

Down to Earth

She and Shamrock had science next and, after saying good-bye to Stella and Celest, headed to the Science Stables.

"I was thinking the Science Stables could inspire an earth element ability," Sapphire was saying.

"Well, you know, I think my photographic memory is related to the earth element. When I look at my memories, they all feel connected to living things, if that makes sense," Shamrock said.

"Actually, it does." Sapphire said, her investigator brain turning on. "How does the picture look when you see it? It is like a photograph? Or a painting?"

Shamrock thought about it. "It's like a photograph in the middle of the memory and a painting on the sides. Like, when I was looking for the basket of flowers, the flowers were a photograph but the surrounding details were more like a painting. I think it depends on what I'm focusing on. But the basket wasn't really clear. The flowers were much more clear. I think because they're rooted in the earth, you know?"

Sapphire nodded. "Totally." She and Shamrock were always able to understand each other. They just had the same logical brains. And before, they'd also been the only ones without a magical ability. Sapphire was happy for her friend, but she couldn't help feeling a little lonely and a little jealous. Those were new feelings for her, and she didn't like them. They felt sticky and uncomfortable. But it was like stepping into quicksand. She didn't know how to shake them off.

★

Professor Sherbet had just sent the science class to start working on their projects when she spotted Sapphire and

Shamrock walking toward the greenhouses. "Hi, you two!" she called.

"Stella and Celest sent word that you guys were on your way. Sounds like you had an extra lesson today." Professor Sherbet smiled at them.

The two students nodded. "Sapphire learned how to

make fire," Shamrock said. "I'm still figuring it out."

Sapphire wasn't paying attention. She was staring hard at the plants in front of her, biting her bottom lip the way she always did when hatching a plan.

"Sapphire? Hello?" Professor Sherbet waved her horn, gently shaking the moss crown on her head.

Sapphire was shaken out of her thoughts. "Sorry, Professor. I've been on a quest today. Would it be okay if Shamrock and I did a separate project right now? I have a burning question."

Professor Sherbet never could say no to a burning question. Like all the first years, Sapphire knew that the professor valued curiosity above all other things. The professor laughed, knowing too that all her students had learned how to pull at her heartstrings. "Oh, go ahead, you two. But I would like a full report of this quest at the end of the day, Sapphire."

Sapphire and Shamrock headed out of the greenhouse. She was feeling hopeful again.

"Don't you want to look at all the cools plants in there?" Shamrock asked.

Sapphire explained, "Remember Peppermint's story about waking up with her mother's knitting wrapped around her because she'd wanted a blanket?"

Shamrock nodded.

"And you developed your ability when Twilight, your friend, was in trouble."

"But I'm not sure where you're going with all this," he admitted.

"As unicorns, we are all connected to the earth. I mean, most of us have to walk on it, after all," Sapphire said. "So I think the earth element, for us anyway, has to do with what's familiar."

Shamrock nodded but his eyebrows were scrunched up, like he didn't quite get it.

"Well remember how I'm learning to weave new nets for Mom? She harvests seaweed and it feels like we're always having to repair the nets. I've been studying the books Mr. Jazz found on the strongest thread and weaving techniques and I started practicing the new weave with ivy and bark. I'm making them for my family so they're personal, and I was thinking maybe they could inspire some magic!"

Shamrock was now nodding in his usual enthusiastic way. "Sapphire, I think this is an important scientific discovery!"

With that, the two set off for the Silver Lining Stables at a friendly canter. Fast enough to get there quickly but slow enough to talk.

"What were you thinking about on the way to the Science Stables?" Sapphire asked. "Obviously you have something on your mind."

"I was actually thinking about that picture day," Shamrock said with a laugh. "I was using my ability to see it again. All that powdered sugar falling onto Twilight like snow. Comet a blur flying above her with that giant bag. It looked like a cloud. It was so fun to relive it all. And you were right, it wasn't sticky at all."

Sapphire cocked her head in confusion. Shamrock hadn't been at the bottom of the hill that day. She and Shamrock had helped Comet carry the bag of powdered sugar before she'd run up the hill with it to get her flying start. Twilight had described it in great detail, of course. But they hadn't actually seen the powdered sugar fall. Sapphire wanted to ask Shamrock questions, but before she had a chance, they saw Comet and Twilight racing toward them.

8

An Emergency

Comet and Twilight looked totally panicked as they rushed up them. Twilight's hooves were shimmering in and out of invisibility, and Comet was hovering over the ground.

"What's wrong?" Sapphire and Shamrock asked in unison. But no one laughed at the coincidence.

Instead Twilight squeaked, "Headmaster Starblaze has called for an emergency meeting on the Looping Lawn."

"Professor Sherbet told us you guys were doing a special project and to come get you right away," Comet explained.

"It's something to do with Fairy Green," Twilight added, her voice full of worry.

With that, the four unicorns cantered as fast as they could toward the Looping Lawn. Had something happened to their honored guest?

They arrived to see the whole campus gathered together in front of the large oak trees. Fairy Green's welcome banner still hung between them, making the whole thing seem sadder.

The teachers all flanked the headmaster, and Sapphire looked up to find Fairy Green perched atop Professor Sherbet's head, leaning back against her horn. She looked at home surround by the moss wreath, but her face was contorted with worry. Sapphire felt like something was missing, but what was it?

Headmaster Starblaze cleared his throat, and the whole university quieted down. "As most of you know," he began in his booming voice, "Unicorn U has had the great honor of hosting Fairy Green today." He paused and nodded toward the fairy, who bowed her small head in return.

"But a grave thing has happened during her time here," the headmaster continued. "Her basket of fairy dust has gone missing."

Sapphire felt tears well up. That basket was Fairy Green's most valuable possession. How would she get home without it? How would she travel? Sapphire wanted to help but didn't know how. *What can a first-year unicorn with no magic do?* Meanwhile, the school had erupted with chatter:

"Has someone taken it?"

"Where could it be?"

"I just saw her with it hours ago!"

"Who would've done such a thing?"

The headmaster stomped his front legs with such force that it felt as if the ground shook beneath them. The students immediately quieted.

"This fairy dust is not of use to unicorns, but it is of serious importance to fairies. Without this basket, Fairy Green will not be able to attend the annual Fairy Gathering, the most important day of the fairies' year. If anyone knows anything about this basket's whereabouts, please see one of your professors immediately. In the meantime, I have formed a search party of teachers. All students are to stay here on the lawn or in the Silver Lining Stables until the dinner bell. Classes have been canceled."

The professors gathered their classes together, doing their best to quiet the gossip and questions. With Fairy Green still perched on top of her head, Professor Sherbet led her students to a tree and asked her class to please wait quietly there while she and Fairy Green checked in with the headmaster. Somehow, Fairy Green seemed to have shrunk with sadness. The class did as they were told. They felt very protective of their fairy guest, and wanted to make her life easier.

But when the adults walked away, a discussion soon started up again.

"We need to do something!" Firefly shouted.

"Of course, but what can a bunch of first years do?" Peppermint asked.

"Well, remember what Flash said earlier today?" Storm asked. "We're the best first years she's seen. We have the best abilities, remember?"

Most of the class nodded in agreement, but some still argued that they should do as they were told.

Now Sapphire really felt she had nothing to offer Fairy Green or her classmates. It was clear the students with magical abilities were going to save the day, and she still hadn't found her magic. *I should get on with my quest,* she thought. Even if it was feeling less and less like she would ever find what she was looking for.

9

Hatching a Plan

Sapphire! Come back!"

Sapphire turned to see her fellow students waving their horns her way. She sighed. *They probably just feel bad for me.*

Sapphire trotted back over to tell them not to worry about her, but her classmates didn't give her the chance.

"Um, where are you going?" Peppermint whined with a spectacular mane flip.

Sapphire took a deep breath and said, "Well, it's clear you don't need me, so—"

"Excuse me!" Comet said, floating slightly up from the ground. "You have been interrupting me all day, but I am going to say what I, and everyone else has been trying to say. We absolutely *do* need you. You're the glue!"

Sapphire rolled her eyes. She was sick of everyone trying to make her feel better. It actually made her angry. She just couldn't take it anymore.

Hot tears welled up as she yelled, "Ugh! You guys obviously do not need me. I have NO magic. I can't fly around campus and look for the basket from the air, like you, Comet. I can't listen in on conversations to see if anyone really did take the basket, like you can, Twilight. I can't call the wind to sweep back the long grass and see if it's hidden in there, like you can, Storm. And I definitely can't take down everyone's memories from the day and use my ability to see when the basket went missing, like you can, Shamrock!" Sapphire finished her rant. She was panting now. All her angry energy had been expelled, like she'd let out all the air from a balloon and was just deflated. She needed a nap. But when she looked up at her classmates, she saw them all smiling at her. "What?" she snapped. Had they not heard her?

It was Twilight who was brave enough to come closer

to the fuming Sapphire. "Well, it seems like you might have a plan for how to save the day. Want to walk us through it? Um, perhaps a bit more calmly and slowly this time?" Twilight smiled and, so only Sapphire could see, winked.

It took Sapphire a minute to work out what Twilight meant. "Well, let's start with Shamrock," she said, a little hesitantly.

"Yeah, what in the kingdoms were you talking about?" he asked.

"Well, I think you might be able to patch together memories that aren't yours into your . . . What did you call it? Memory movie?"

Shamrock nodded.

"Okay, well, I was thinking of when you told me about reliving the time when Comet poured powdered sugar all over Twilight. You actually didn't see that, remember? We were on the other side of the hill. But Twilight told us about it. I think you were able to access her memory when she shared it somehow, and add it to the movie."

It was like the class was watching a hoofball match. As soon as Sapphire stopped talking, they all turned to Shamrock at once, wondering if it was true.

Shamrock's glasses shook up and down his nose as he nodded, taking in what she was saying. "Oh my glitter, you're right! And if enough unicorns tell me exactly when and where they saw Fairy Green, I should be able to put together a mental movie of the day!"

It seemed both sides had won this match, as the whole

class cheered together. Everyone gathered in a line, eager to share their stories with Shamrock.

When the class had finished, Shamrock closed his eyes. Breathing in and out, he took his time putting the memories together. Finally he opened his eyes to look at everyone. But he had a heavy frown, and his eyebrows were pushed low enough to be entirely hidden by his glasses. It didn't seem as if he had succeeded.

Sapphire, who was starting to feel like her old self again, walked over with confidence. "Think about the earth," she suggested. "Think about the trees and flowers and grass included in their memories. Think painting, not movie."

Shamrock smiled at her, and closed his eyes again. The class waited silently for what felt like hours but was only a few minutes. Then Shamrock opened his eyes. This time triumph was shining through.

"Okay," Shamrock said. "It seems that no one has seen the basket since Fairy Green flew over the Spotlight Flowers. That was when she was also carrying a bunch of baskets from Stella and Celest, so it would make sense if she didn't notice one of them drop."

Sapphire smiled, picking up where he was going. "And since Spotlight Flowers close whenever someone is near, they may have closed up right over the basket."

The class cheered again. They'd figured it out!

"Um, excuse me!" Peppermint called out. "Does no one else see the problem? The Spotlight Garden is humungous. How is Twilight supposed to search the area all by herself? And I'm pretty sure she's the only invisible unicorn in the whole school."

"Actually, I have a plan for that," Sapphire said. She grinned, and her friends noticed that the sparkle in her eye was back. And it might just have been bigger than ever.

10

A Search Party

Sapphire, Comet, Twilight, and Shamrock got ready for their new quest. Students were supposed to be staying on the Looping Lawn, so this was going to have to be a covert mission. A herd of first years was not going to go unnoticed.

Before the group left, Peppermint wove a long length of ivy around Comet's waist. She even wove some flowers through it, making it almost as beautiful as her welcome banner. "What?" Peppermint asked when she saw Sapphire's face. "Just because it's practical doesn't mean it has to be boring."

Sapphire just shrugged.

When everyone was ready, Sapphire gave Storm the signal—two stomps and a whinny.

Storm called up a wicked wind and whipped it into a small tornado. The spiral wiggled through the lawn, drawing everyone's attention. Just like it was supposed to.

Sapphire and her rescue team made their escape. Keeping off the main paths, and sticking to the woods, they made their way to the Spotlight Garden.

✦

"Okay, Fairy Green was seen flying into the Spotlight Garden from this side, so I think we should start here. She was next seen at the Science Stables, so head in that direction, Twilight," Shamrock told her.

Sapphire handed Twilight one end of the ivy. The other was still tied around Comet's waist. "Hold this in your mouth, Twilight, and be careful not to let it touch the ground."

"Okay," Twilight said, looking nervous about the important part she had to play.

"You can totally do this," Sapphire assured her.

Twilight smiled at Sapphire before she closed her eyes, and soon enough she disappeared from view. Even though they'd seen it a million times by now, her friends were always astounded at how good she was at disappearing. She was really starting to master this ability. *A long way from the first day,* Sapphire thought.

"Here I go," invisible Twilight told them, her voice muffled by the ivy rope.

"Then I guess that's my cue," Comet said. She was

already floating in excitement, so she just pedaled her legs as if she were swimming in air, and rose higher. Soon she was well above the other unicorns' heads.

"Comet! Stop pedaling. Let Twilight pull you. Just focus on finding the basket!" Sapphire reminded her.

"Right-o, Captain!" Comet yelled from above, and she did start searching below.

Sapphire and Shamrock waited nervously, both wiggling in anticipation, until finally Comet called, "Twilight! Twilight! Turn around and walk three steps back. There's the basket!"

And just moments later, Fairy Green's bark basket was floating over the Spotlight Flowers as Comet flew above.

"You know, it's really quite something to see the world from up here," Comet called down to them all.

11

The Fairy Good Return

The students on the Looping Lawn greeted the four friends with big cheers. Some older students even started the chant "Best first years ever!"

But the teachers did not seem to be in the same mood. Even Professor Sherbet looked disappointed. "You should not have done that on your own," she told them in a very serious voice. "You should always tell a teacher."

"Your teacher is right. It is important to listen to your elders," Fairy Green added, still sitting on Professor Sherbet's head.

All at once Sapphire, Shamrock, Twilight, and Comet started talking.

"It was all in the name of the school," Shamrock tried to argue.

"Please don't be angry! Please, please, please!" Comet pleaded.

Twilight mumbled something no one could understand.

It was Sapphire who stepped forward calmly. "It was my idea, Professor," she said with her head held high. Her heart was beating wildly and she wanted to bite her lip. But she willed herself to stand up for their plan, and protect her friends. She looked first into the eyes of Professor Sherbet. "It was my plan, Professor, the whole thing." Then, though it felt as if her body were frozen in fear, she turned toward the headmaster. "None of the other students should be punished. I convinced them to do it." And finally, even though it now felt as if Storm had sent icy rain to keep her from looking up, Sapphire made herself look into Fairy Green's eyes to say, "I think your class today may have changed my whole life. And I didn't want you to think badly about our school. And I didn't want you to miss the gathering. So I don't regret what we did. I'm happy you have your basket again."

Fairy Green and Professor Sherbet smiled at Sapphire with such warmth that they made her feel like they'd asked the sun to melt all that ice away and fill her up with sunshine.

But the headmaster did not seem at all moved by her words. "Please come to my office, Sapphire." He turned without even looking to make sure she followed him.

"After you speak with your headmaster," Fairy Green told her, "I do hope we can have a chance to talk before I leave."

Sapphire could only stare in wonder at such an opportunity. If she had to get through a lecture to talk to Fairy Green, she would. That gave her all the bravery she needed. With a deep breath, Sapphire squared her shoulders and followed the headmaster.

The headmaster's office was not the scary place she'd expected. She didn't know what exactly she *had* expected, but it wasn't this cozy room. There wasn't even a desk! Just a large rug and a fireplace. The walls were lined with book hooks and paintings of all different sizes and in all different styles of art. The books too seemed to be a mix of things.

There were fantasy stories and textbooks, dictionaries and thrillers. *Who is this unicorn?* Sapphire wondered.

"Are you ready now?"

Sapphire jumped back a little. She hadn't realized how long she'd been staring at his things. "Oh, um, yes, Headmaster, sir," she said as confidently as she could manage.

Headmaster Starblaze surprised her even further by chuckling softly. "Now, now, you're not in trouble, Sapphire. In fact, I would like to thank you."

"But, Headmaster. Before—it seemed, well, like you were going to expel me."

"You did break the rules. You and your fellow first years will have to receive some sort of punishment. I'll think on that. But for now I'd like to offer my thanks. Your search party proved much more successful than mine. And I do believe you have helped the five kingdoms because of it."

"Well, thank you, sir," Sapphire said, feeling about a million times better. She wanted to tell him it was all because of her classmates' abilities, but she didn't want to get them

in any more trouble. Plus, she was beginning to realize that she'd played a big part in finding the basket. Perhaps the biggest of all.

"Okay, that is all. You may rejoin your friends, Sapphire."

Sapphire turned to go, but, curiosity getting the best of her, she turned back around and asked, "Headmaster, what's your ability?"

The headmaster looked taken aback. "No one has ever asked me before," he said.

Sapphire laughed. He was the third person to say that to her that day.

"Well, since no one knows, all the students think it must be something very impressive. Or terrible."

The headmaster threw back his head and laughed so hard, the picture frames shook on the walls. When he finally stopped, he said, "I don't have an ability, Sapphire. It's just me."

"You know what? I don't think I have one either," Sapphire admitted, and she turned around and left the office. She skipped all the way out, feeling lighter than air.

✳

Before she got back to the Looping Lawn, Sapphire saw Fairy Green flying her way. The fairy had her basket securely over her shoulder and was carrying a tiny suitcase. "Sapphire!" she called out.

Sapphire went over to her. The dancing beans from earlier felt like they had found their way back to her hooves. She skidded to a stop in front of the fairy, catching herself from falling just in time.

"I wanted to clarify my answer from this morning, Sapphire," Fairy Green said.

Sapphire hadn't been expecting that. She could only blink in surprise.

"I want you to know that you have magic, Sapphire. And certainly enough to travel the five kingdoms. Magic comes in so many forms. Sometimes as dust. Sometimes as flashy unicorn abilities. And sometimes it comes in the form of leadership, curiosity, or a good heart. And you have all three of those."

Sapphire was speechless. It was the kindest thing anyone

had ever said. "Uh—thank you, Fairy Green," she finally managed.

"Oh, and that's the other thing. My real name is 'Juniper.' Now that you know it, you can call on me and I'll hear it wherever I am. If you ever need me, just say my name and I'll find you."

"Thank you very much, Juniper. I am honored," Sapphire said, tears of pride brimming in her eyes.

And with that, Juniper sprinkled some fairy dust and disappeared with a pop.

Sapphire looked up to see her friends waving from up on the hill. Looking at them, she realized that it wasn't their abilities that made them special. Not at all. They were magical because of the unicorns they were. Sapphire took out her notebook and wrote "Magic found" and underlined it.

Smiling, she galloped over to her friends and wondered what kind of adventure they were going to go on next.

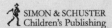

READ& LEARN

with

simon kids

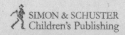

SIMON & SCHUSTER
Children's Publishing